The
Perfect Prayer

DONALD ROSSOFF

Illustrated by
TAMMY L. KEISER

UAHC Press · New York, New York

Dedicated in love
to Fran and to Marc,
Jenna, Ilana, and Nathaniel...
the answers to my prayers
— DR

To Ian and Ari
with love
— TK

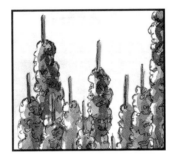

Library of Congress Cataloging-in-Publication Data

Rossoff, Donald.
    The perfect prayer/ Donald Rossoff ; illustrated by Tammy L. Keiser.
        p. cm.
    Summary: When a queen needs a perfect prayer, her three advisors suggest sounds for
listening, thinking, and wondering, and the queen combines them to come up with "Shema."
    ISBN 0-8074-0853-0 (cloth : alk. paper)
    1. Jews--Juvenile fiction. [1. Jews--Fiction. 2. Prayer--Fiction.] I. Keiser, Tammy L. II.
Title.

PZ7.R7288Pe 2003
[Fic]--dc21

                                                                                        2002043580

There once was a queen who needed a prayer.

She needed a prayer, for there wasn't one there.
So she called to her advisors to give her advice.

"Come, my advisors," she said. "Help me discover the sounds of a perfect prayer, a prayer that will open us to God."

The first advisor, Shimon, came forward.

"Your Highness," he said, "the sound of your prayer should be 'shhhhh.' Not only is 'shhh' the sound of the ocean kissing the shore and the wind whispering through the trees, 'shhh,'" holding his finger to his lips, "is the sound that asks us to listen."

"The world is filled with so many sounds that distract us. 'Shhh' helps us listen for the voice of our deepest feelings, the voice of God within us. I think the perfect prayer should go 'shhh.'"

And the other advisors nodded their heads, smiled, and said, "Yes!"

The next advisor, Miriam, came forward and said, "I think Your Majesty's prayer should have the sound 'mmmmm.' 'Mmmm,'" resting her chin between her thumb and her forefinger, "is the sound of thinking."

"In prayer, I think about the really important things. I think about myself, about others, about the world, and I think about how God ties everything all together. 'Mmmm' is the sound of insight and understanding. 'Mmmm,'" said Miriam, "is, for me, the sound of the perfect prayer."

And the other two advisors nodded their heads, smiled, and said, "Yes!"

The third advisor's name was Akiva.

"For me," said Akiva, "the perfect prayer needs to have the sound 'ahhh.' 'Ahhh,'" holding both hands up, "is the sound of wonder and awe. I look at the world around me and see how amazing it is, so complicated and yet so simple. So much intricate beauty! So much overwhelming majesty."

"Then I look at the world that is me, my mind, my body, my spirit, and I marvel at the wonder that is me and that is everything else that God makes! Wow—everywhere I go, God is there, too!"

"And when I realize that God is the One in whose oneness
are all things one, the only sound I can make is 'ahhh!'"
     And once again, the other advisors nodded their heads,
smiled, and said, "Yes!"

Then the three advisors, Shimon, Miriam, and Akiva, looked up at the Queen, wondering which sound she would pick, hoping that the prayer she chose would be theirs.

But the Queen's head was bowed in thought. Finally, after what seemed to be a long time, she raised her head slowly, looked at them squarely, and said, "Each of you have spoken with understanding, and together you have spoken with wisdom."

"You have taught me that the very best prayers have us listen, have us think, have us wonder. My prayer will unite all three of your sounds: Shimon's 'shhh,' Miriam's 'mmmm,' and Akiva's 'ahhh,' and together these sounds will speak the prayer of my heart."

"That's it!" said the Queen.

"The sound of our perfect prayer will be 'Sh'ma!'"

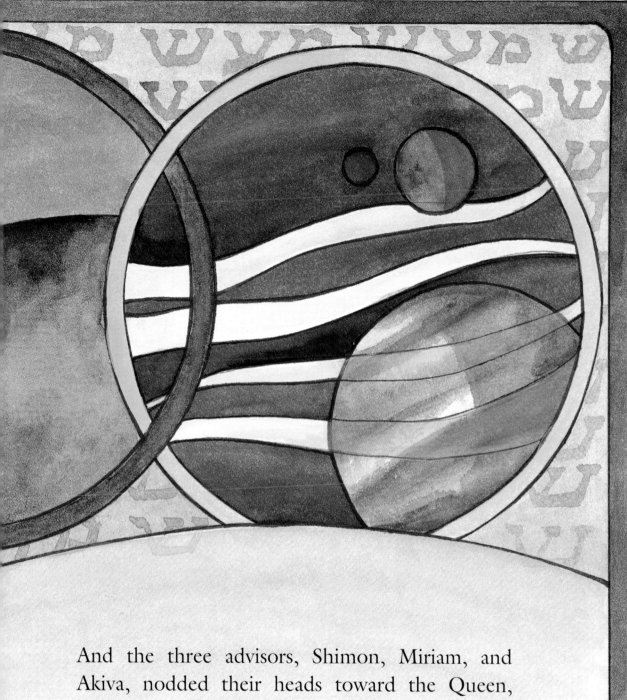

And the three advisors, Shimon, Miriam, and Akiva, nodded their heads toward the Queen, nodded their heads toward each other, and smiling three very big smiles, said, "Yes!!"

שְׁמַע יִשְׂרָאֵל יְיָ אֱלֹהֵינוּ יְיָ אֶחָד:

Sh'ma Yisrael, Adonai Eloheinu, Adonai Echad.

Hear O Israel, Adonai is Our God, Adonai is One.

Notes on the *Sh'ma*

The prayer we call by its first word, "*Sh'ma,*" is a doorway to meaning and connection. Thousands of pages of interpretation have been written about these six simple words taken from the Torah (Deuteronomy 6:4). It is these words that Jews of spirit pronounce daily in liturgical moments and at night before sleep. It is these words that are the last on our lips as we die and join God's immortality. Some have called it the Jewish pledge of allegiance.

The *Sh'ma* is not a prayer to God. It is a declarative statement about God, about us, and about the connections binding us with God and with each other. It is a proclamation of the Jewish people to the Jewish people and to all peoples that there is but one God, that God is one, that God is #1, and that in God's oneness are all peoples, all persons, and all things one.

PAST

In saying "*Sh'ma Yisrael*—Listen Israel," we address our patriarch Israel/Jacob, who, according to the Midrash, is concerned on his deathbed that the faith of his parents and grandparents will die with him. Thus we, his decendants, say to him, "Listen, (Father) Israel, your faith has not died. The covenant between your children and the God of your fathers and mothers is living through us and our children!"

PRESENT

In saying "*Sh'ma Yisrael*—Listen Israel," Jews call each other to community, linked to all other Jews as the people Israel wherever they live in the common bonds of faith and fate. In speaking of *our* God, the Jew asserts the "we-ness" of that "meta-*mishpachah*" (transcendent family) we call the Jewish people and affirms his or her part in that collective "we."

Together, we proclaim that *Adonai,* the One whose true ineffable name implies Being Itself, is *Eloheinu,* our God, ours not in a possessive sense but in a most personal sense. We can know God personally, through the many names given to God by those who came before us and through the names we ourselves give, revealed through our own individual and collective experience of the Divine within us, around us, and above us.

FUTURE

In saying "*Sh'ma Yisrael*—Listen Israel," we pledge our commitment to carrying on the covenant between God and the Jewish people. We work to continue that covenant by learning and living Torah as we understand it; by passing it down to the next generation, through our own children or by being part of institutions that do; by supporting the Jewish people living in the State of Israel; and by working, through our doing and our giving, to bring the world closer to what God dreams it to be.

Author's Note

The seed of *The Perfect Prayer* was planted when I heard a *d'rash* (interpretation of Torah) on the word *Sh'ma* connecting the sound "sh" with the act of listening, the sound "m" with the act of pondering, and the sound "ah" with the experience of wonder.

That seed began to germinate as I was searching for a new story to offer at my temple's Rosh HaShanah family service. I decided to write a midrash (creative interpretation) on that *Sh'ma d'rash*. I formed the outline of the story in my mind and rehearsed it by myself, as diligent storytellers do, but much of the language that appears on these pages was created in the experience of the telling itself. There is something about open ears, open eyes, and open hearts that provide fertile ground for a story to blossom. Thank you, children of Temple B'nai Or, for your ears, eyes, and hearts ever open.

Finally, I thought I understood the story rather well, but when I first saw Tammy L. Keiser's illustrations, I began to comprehend it in ways I had never imagined. I owe great thanks to her for her exquisite and truly illuminating midrash on my midrash on the *d'rash*.

Who the original source of this *d'rash* was, I don't know. The rabbi from whom I remembered learning it said he had never heard of it. I then consulted with a number of my musician and storytelling friends. Many had heard of the *d'rash* and attributed it to various sources, but still I could not track down from whom I had received it.

Maybe, when it comes to an oral legend such as this, the origin is less important than the transmission. As Craig Taubman perceptibly wrote to me, "Perhaps that is the beauty of this *d'rash* . . . it is not in the telling nor in attribution, but in the hearing!"

Rabbi Donald Rossoff, R.J.E.
Morristown, New Jersey